MAD VIGILANCE

A STORY WITHIN THE MAD UNIVERSE

ISBN: 979-8-9859259-0-6

BEFORE YOU READ

'Stories in the MAD Universe' are a series of supplementary pieces that take place within the MAD Series. While *Mad Vigilance* is the first tie-in novella, it is **NOT** the first entry in the MAD series.

The first book is the novel known as *Mad City*. If you've already read *Mad City*, then fantastic! Please move on and enjoy the rest of this novella.

If you have not read *Mad City*, it is highly essential to read *Mad City* first before *Mad Vigilance* so that you can have a full understanding of the story ahead. You can grab a copy by scanning the QR code below.

Happy Reading! ~Victor Vahl

PROLOGUE

Isaac Sage

October 5, 2023 // 2:33 AM

Rigid ink lines formed together an imperfect silhouette. The only complement being the pale moonlight, over-exposing the outline. Isaac's torso hunched over, creating hills from clenched fabric. His whole body was further restrained by thick braids of rope.

Rasps of air escaped Isaac's helmet. Static accumulated as a line of restrained thugs, adjacent to both sides of him, died one by one. Pop. Pop. Pop. That was the sounds of their heads exploding.

Parts of his nerves reminded him he was still alive. The welted bruises scattered across his body pulsated, some stacked of blue and purple and black, while the darkened red cuts stung. In-between, his body was stained with naturally healed scars.

The uneven scatter resembled the wild swings of a loaded paintbrush against a canvas. His eyes paled against the moonlight.

———

But now, the nerve that rung most was his heart, racing as the popping sounds grew closer, the dull canvas surrounding Isaac transforming into a crimson bloodbath. Even at the peak of his physical performance, and having raided warehouses consistently for 6 months, here he was: A hostage, beaten down and tied up.

Every past event led to this moment. Geared up in his black military-grade boots, slate camo pants, grey hoodie, and black helmet. Across from him stood a lanky teenager, accompanied by an older man, just an inch shorter than the teen.

The teenager's arms were stretched out, moving to each combusting head like the arm on a clock. The arms would eventually reach Isaac.

What was the first impulse? For his life to flash before his eyes. The pain, the suffering, the few light moments in-between. Was this the intended fate for him? Dying in a building where no one would find him? He would practically vanish off the face of the earth.

Finally, all his mind did was reflect. Back to earlier, awaking foggy-headed and meeting the friend that would compel him to question the current path he was on.

I

TODD ANDERSON

October 3, 2023 // 11:15 AM

The men seated in front of Todd were all nothing but dots. Blurred into a kaleidoscope-like array of colors, vibrant and dull overlapping, mingling underneath fluorescent lights. They were also the ones to decide Todd's fate moving forward.

4 months ago, Todd applied for early graduation in his bachelor's program. A month after, he began his master's program, kickstarting his dissertation.

The concept behind the dissertation was a set of specialized climate ribbons that promoted safe energy through wind, water, and electricity simultaneously. It was inspired by the climate ribbons used to funnel air in the Brickell City Centre in Miami.

The following months after, Todd simultaneously pursued pitch interviews with several tech companies. His focus: the nanobots.

The nanobots he built several months ago had the function to improve the human body without any chemical alteration, or medicinal insertion. It would sustain life longer and be the natural way for any person to live their life to the fullest without a single ounce of concern.

He knew what he had was potential to change the world, just like how M.A.D. changed the world. All he needed was for someone to listen to his speech and believe in him enough to invest in this project for mass production.

Out of the hundreds he applied to, from corporate-sized to start-up, only 11 agreed to arrange a meeting with him.

And with 10 pitches, there was no success. Either the owners went silent or acknowledged to Todd that the company would be moving in a different direction. With the rejection of every meeting, Todd re-crafted the tone of his pitch, and made sure the guts of his content were just as interesting as the hook.

Permanent robotics that can keep a human healthy without the constant insertion of medicine. 'Who wouldn't want that?' Todd thought.

———

He ran through every pitch meeting in tunnel vision. "No matter what, do as rehearsed," he told himself before every meeting, "Don't branch off. It doesn't matter who's looking. It's all a fucking stage play at this point. State the financials, Cover the purpose. Briefly go over specs. State the long-term goals, and budget. Numbers, numbers, numbers."

Todd learned quickly that the numbers is where every company, big or small, reacted the most through expression alone. Where he stood now, in front of the men-in-suits of LyonsMane embodying his 11th pitch meeting, the finale of Todd's speech was met with silent reciprocation.

"So, any questions?" Todd asked, hoping his crowd was too shy to show their excitement over his invention.

In unison, the men-in-suits stood up and proceeded to the exit doorway. "None at all," Willa Lyons, the owner of LyonsMane, rose from the rear center seat. Her fiery gold hair alone shouted from across the room. "Thank you, Todd." In swift fashion, she exited the room.

Todd sighed, and gathered his folders, ready to depart. Lyons' assistant, Rufus, approached Todd. Rufus was Todd's main point of contact for arranging this meeting. Curly hair frizzed out of control around his spectacles.

"Hey Todd, I just wanted to say your pitch was fantastic."

"Thanks," Todd smiled, "Maybe you should've applauded to get the rest of them going."

Rufus scratched the back of his head, "I guess so. I'll talk to Willa to see where her head's at. Maybe do some refinement."

"Please do," said Todd, trying to hide any hint of frustration in his voice. He continued stowing his documents into his brown leather computer satchel, before departing, towards the exit opposite of where his audience marched towards.

He stepped out to grey skies cast over the concrete tower. The frustration festered up. 11 pitch meetings, and he couldn't nail one. 'Maybe do some refinement.' Todd continued repeating that line in his head.

Todd dug from the pit of his lungs and roared to the point of scratching his vocal cords. He wound back his right arm, fist clenched, catapulting it against the concrete wall like the snap of a rubber band.

There was no care over how many bones Todd broke, or even if people heard him. In fact, he would've relished in leaving a dent. Instead, all he left were blood stains in the shape of his knuckles.

From the corner of his eye, Rufus stood at the doorway. His mouth slightly agape, locking eyes at Todd. Todd wasn't sure if he was in awe or terrified. Or both.

Todd cleared his throat, hiding his bloodied hand. "Any good spots to eat here?"

"Um, there's a great ceviche joint that just opened. Oh, but I normally get food from the taco bar nearby. They have great deals on Fridays and Tuesdays. Because y'kno, Taco Tuesdays"-

"Right, I get it," Todd chuckled nervously. "I guess I'll give that a try."

Rufus extended his right hand with a half-bright smirk. "Let me know what you think, and I just wanted to come out and re-affirm we'll keep in touch about this project."

Hesitant, Todd extended out his bloodied hand to shake Rufus'. The adrenaline died down, as the bones in his hand ached in burning excruciation. Todd did his best to keep his hand from trembling uncontrollably. He refrained from wincing too much in pain.

But Rufus was smart. His eyes hung low with genuine

worry, but he continued to maintain his professionalism. At the same time, Rufus could've walked away and chosen to not even speak to Todd. Instead, he reacted to him with kindness and understanding.

Rufus leaned further into Todd, the air escaping from the former's mouth close to Todd's ear. "I should have you know that I think Willa has nothing against your work, or your pitch."

Todd squinted his eyes. This was only his third conversation with Rufus. "Where's this coming from?" Todd asked. "You said it needed refining."

"From a good place of mind, I just can't brush you off like that and lie. She's only taken me once to some warehouse disguised as a commerce building in the Bronx. The blackout zone." Rufus shuddered from the corner of Todd's eye, as if revealing that sliver of information brought a sense of relief from his own conscience.

"Right," Todd said, slightly stifling in pain. "Well, I guess I'll keep searching in the meantime. Thank you for your honesty, Rufus."

Rufus leaned back, and with a smile, finished shaking Todd's hand. "The pleasure is all mine." Todd proceeded to the exit.

If only, he thought, if only there were more people like Mr. Gallagher that showed keen interest in Todd's nano-bots. Although, suspicions still laid for the whereabouts of Todd's first nanobot since he lost it at the subway platform 6 months ago.

That problem, however, was not going to help him reach his goals. It was something to think about for another day.

* * *

Deep breaths and affirmations of "'tis but a small wound" were Todd's method in reducing the pain in his hand. Logically, it was most likely broken. But Todd refused to go to a hospital and be billed an outrageous amount.

He exhaled through gritted teeth. 'This is fine,' Todd thought, 'This is fine.'

Light cracked through sheets of grey skies, as Todd en-joyed two tacos laid atop a paper-laced steel tray. He shift-ed his gaze to all the passersby grouped in pairs, trios, or alone but talking on their phones.

———

Todd focused a lot of time on himself, fueled with conviction to see something grand come out of his work. A result that would propel him to success. The method to get there was work and study.

He always told himself deep down that once the work and research was over, he would return home to his family. Todd would have the knowledge and experience to open his own business there, and become financially at peace

Isaac was moving toward his own ideals, as was himself and Rosemary, whom Todd hadn't heard from in months. Other friends were nothing but a figment in his memories.

In all these months, however, he was alone. He yearned for company. He called his mother, Jodi. The phone rung once before her voice emerged from the other line. Her voice was as he remembered: soft, yet rough like smooth brass with a ribbed texture. "Do my eyes deceive me?" were Jodi's first words.

"It's me, mom," Todd replied.

"Oh my God," Jodi's tone brightened. "I'll need to tell my co-workers that the Todd Anderson called."

Todd laughed. "How you been, mom? How's everyone?"

"Same ol' same ol' over here, sweetie."

"That's good," Todd took a gulp of air, unsure of what
to say next. "Really good."

"How are you, sweetie? Are you fine in the city? Bills
aren't catching up? Eating well?"

"All of that's good, I've just…I've been keeping to
myself." A weight lifted off Todd's chest. He could finally
talk about his past concerns instead of keeping them locked
within his thoughts for so long. "I miss you all."

"Oh no, no, no," the tone of concern raised in Jodi's
voice. "Why alone? What about the friends you made?
What about Isaac?" Jodi gasped. "Don't tell me you two
hate each other now?"

"We had a disagreement, but we're good now, mom.
He's just doing his own things."

"You should still force your way to check in on him.
You know that boy's history, the poor thing."

"I will, when I'm done focusing on my own stuff."

———

"Have you been sleeping better? Your father was telling me some months ago you were getting some bad insomnia."

Todd reflected on those insomnia bouts. The voices in his head vanished one day, to his blissful relief. But the anger lingered. And in exchange for the voices, came dreams of standing in a sea of black tar in a white room.

Unable to look nor turn back, to only keep moving forward, as the tar rose to his mouth and nostrils. Soon after, his body would thrash and flail around to no success. The suffocation stung him so much that the pain lingered into reality when he snapped awake.

Todd wasn't going to worry his mother by sharing all the details. "My sleeping is better," he said while exhaling through gritted teeth, comforting his hand. "8 good hours of sleep."

"Are you close to graduating? I keep fighting against your father on turning your room into a leisure sort of thing."

"Leisure?"

"Like a gym. Or another office."

"Well, don't."

"So, are you close then?"

"No, I just started my masters."

"Gym it is. Or a gym office. You'll have a nice tread-mill next to your bed when you're back home."

Todd laughed over the thought of waking up to his father heaving in and out while stomping against the tread-mill. "I was trying to patent one of my inventions with a company. Didn't work out."

"One step at a time, sweetie. You have your masters. Focus on that, and everything will fall in place."

All his mother's words resonated and came from a genuine place of hope and optimism. They reminded him of the times she comforted and scolded him as a child. The words that shaped him into the man he is today. "I think I'll just focus on that, yeah," he reiterated Jodi's words. "You're right."

"Of course, I'm right. Your father was very quick to learn that."

"Say, mom, when I do get home, do you think…" Todd flustered at the thought, staring down at his unfinished tacos. "Do you think you could make me my favorite dish?"

"The potato chicken salad? Of course."

Todd's eyes welled up for a split-second. The thought of living with his families for the next few years, not having to worry about his career or a lonely meal brought warmth and peace.

Before he became overwhelmed with his emotions, he closed the call with his mother. "Mom, I gotta go. I'll talk to you later, okay? I love you."

"Okay. I love you too, sweetie. Please don't be a stranger."

"I'll try," Todd said softly. "Bye."

Todd hung up. He switched over to the news app, scrolling through while enjoying the rest of his food. Sage Foundations was influencing the stock market, slowly rising adjacent medical suppliers. In turn, it was bringing a slow climb to the economy.

Other news included the reports of a masked individual roaming the cities of New Manhattan at night. Suspects rumor that this individual is linked to the fires sporadically appearing across the city, originating from random buildings with unconscious suspects.

Those suspects, however, refuse to disclose anything other than a demon attacking them.

Suddenly, Todd noticed a new notification on his phone: an email from his professor overseeing his dissertation.

Todd checked the email. The professor wrote the following:

'Good job on the dissertation so far. I was so intrigued that I forwarded it to a contact at Sage Foundation. They're interested in getting to see more from you. I'll keep you posted on a scheduled slot.'

Todd's neutral expression sparked into pure euphoria. He nearly jumped up from his seat, toppling the steel tray of food left over. It was only a meeting, but it was something Todd figured he was already sidelined from.

He had to celebrate. Get back home, freshen up, and enjoy the rest of the day at home, resting after a long time.

From the conversation with his mom, and the company Todd was prepped to see, he could only think of one friend to celebrate this achievement with tomorrow: Isaac Sage.

———

His right hand winced once again in pain. Todd nearly fell over. His plans changed. First, the hospital.

II

Isaac Sage

October 4, 2023 // 7:30 AM

For the first time in a while, Isaac's routine led him to arriving to work 30 seconds early. He swept his hands through his clean-shaped hair, padding down any signs of fuzzy strands. He checked his reflection, ensuring he remained with a bright-eyed, professional appearance.

With a lack of experience, Sage Foundations handed Isaac entry-level work as a starting point, suggested by Mr. Rudy Vel Gallagher, the new owner of Sage Foundations.

The tasks involved filing reports pertaining to catalogs of logistics, or prototype schematics of certain M.A.D. variations. These variations logged as either botched or moved to a certain phase of planning, to Isaac's understanding. No one ever explained to him what exactly the context of the papers, albeit the intended archive location.

Isaac clocked in, went up to his respective floor, and found a new stack of papers on his desk. The stack nearly glowed thanks to the backdrop of the New Manhattan cityscape beaming through Isaac's office window.

A bright, yellow post-it note popped atop the stack. 'Got a last-minute meeting. Please scan asap - Jerry.'

Work happened to be Isaac's best distraction from constantly thinking about his plans for attacking warehouses. Their leader Diablo died 6 months ago, thanks to the efforts of Isaac and the NMPD.

Ultimately, Isaac wanted Diablo's death. After being done, he could've focused on his engineering career, or his personal life. Traveling with the remaining trust funds he had would be a pleasure, too.

Despite those options, Isaac became a shell. Autonomous, from simple work tasks to mundane events like swiping a card a few times to register correctly, hop on the subway at the last minute, let the wheels grinding against the rusted tracks lull him into a trance, or listen to passersby talk about current events, or shallow gossip.

Even the excitement of the night life, planning for warehouse raids and raiding them slowly sucked the life out of him like a leech.

Before Isaac stopped attending his therapy sessions, Dr.

Bukowski once asked Isaac where he envisioned himself in 5 years. Answering this question now, Isaac felt compelled to say that he was fated to live this cycle.

Maybe this destitution connected what happened to her. Whatever happened to her, because of him.

Every time the thought occurred, only blankness or a grey blur entered his mind, interlaced with the feeling of shock and horror. And yet, to his confusion, it rang not as a living nightmare, but an absolute truth.

It was an action done to someone. To her. Her name was so close to his lips at times. The name that would make his body cave in.

________.

"Hey," a worker signaled Isaac's attention while he stood in front of the scanner, feeding paper as he waited for duplicates to spit out. "Sorry, you almost done?"

"Uh..." Isaac counted the number of papers left. He lost himself in the cycle once again. "Gonna have to give me a few minutes and you can have the machine all to yourself."

"Great, thanks."

After scanning the papers, Isaac sat back down in his

office and refamiliarized himself with how many nameless workers, sans Jerry, swam through this building.

His phone rang. The caller ID showed it was Todd. "Hey man," Isaac immediately answered.

"How's the ever-prominent Sage engineer?" Todd asked brightly.

"Oh, wonderful. They got me engineering papers."

"Holy shit! I sense a promotion."

Isaac laughed. "How've you been? Been a while."

"Well, the master's coming along smoothly as I grow more grey hairs."

"What's wrong with grey hairs?"

"Sorry, did I strike a nerve with your grey hairs? You have them too, don't you?

"Uh…" Isaac stammered over the last time he examined his head of hair.

"Oh man, you do!" Todd chuckled. "You're dying them to some mismatched color, aren't you?"

"I'm gonna hang up, man."

———

"Alright, alright. Look, I'm off class today and I'm in the area. You wanna grab a bite?"

Isaac stared at the time, and the incomplete stack of papers. Fuck it. "I could kill some time."

"Alright! Let's meet at Sticky's."

* * *

Isaac and Todd sat down in the booth after making their order. The small restaurant rung with vibrancy through its red and yellow palette.

"Haven't had this in a while," said Isaac, "Great choice."

"Best chicken tenders around in New Manhattan, and I'll fight that to my grave. I mean, check out this sauce," Todd scooped up a dab of a pink peppered sauce with his tongue.

"Maybe actually wait for the food? Your argument's less convincing when you eat sauce like that, weirdo."

"Look who's talking. I wanted to check if you were doing alright."

Isaac shrugged, "I guess I'm doing fine."

———

21

"No offense, but you look like you've lost days of sleep..."

Isaac sighed, following with a shrug. The last thing he cared about was his appearance, besides looking clean enough for work.

He eyed down at Todd's bandaged hand. "That hand doesn't look so good either."

Todd shrugged. "Yeah, I'm in underground fight clubs now." The bags around his eye-lids became more notice-able, dark, and sunken. "Which is a joke, 100%. I've been studying like a madman."

"We're busy people."

"Yeah, yeah. You got your side projects and all that as do I, I understand," Todd took another bite of his chicken. "Still, bummer. From the way you're looking, you gotta avoid overworking yourself."

"Hey, no need to worry about me," Isaac interjected, twirling around his small cup of ketchup. "I'm fine."

"Yeah?"

The tenders arrived at the table. Warm and crisped in golden brown, served in a greased paper bowl, with all the right texture and savory smell of its spices. Todd and Isaac began eating without a word.

"Well, we might collaborate as work buddies," Todd spoke, covering his full mouth.

"What makes you say that?" Isaac sprayed out a chicken crumb, raising his hand over his mouth. "Sorry."

Todd cleared his throat. "I got a big invention coming up being part of my dissertation. Professors hinted at showcasing the concept to...Sage Foundations."

Isaac nearly choked on his food. He patted his chest, clearing out hiccups of air. "What?! Todd, that's fucking amazing."

"I can't disclose much but...I wanted to let you know what I'm able to share."

"Yeah. Thanks," Isaac bit off a piece of his tender, "Proud of you."

"Yeah, it's been a weird run. I've been on about 11 pitch meetings, and all of them had been rejected. Funny thing though, the last one I was at is apparently illegally suppling M.A.D."

Isaac cleared his throat. "A warehouse supplying

M.A.D.?”

“Yeah,” Todd nodded. He picked at his fries while talking about it. “Again, pretty weird. The assistant helping with arranging the meeting had commented on that. In some commerce building in The Bronx of all places, too.”

“It is inconspicuous.”

Todd raised his brows. “Good point.”

Another good point was to keep a mental note of this warehouse. It was worth checking out, since no warehouse was in The Bronx based on Isaac’s map. Maybe this would lead Isaac elsewhere.

“Hey, you remember the one time- ehehe, hold on,” Todd snickered, regaining his composure, “You remember the one time we snuck out of school, this was like... 5th grade, yeah?”

While his mind was now on the warehouse, and when to strike, Isaac rubbed the temples of his forehead, struggling to remember Todd’s shared memory.

“We managed to get out of the school fence around lunch period, for some reason one of the school guards disappeared from their usual post. We climbed over the fence, and the first thing you said we gotta do was"-

"We gotta return this video game..." Isaac continued from Todd's speech. The memory slowly bled back in his mind. "Because the game was so bad it burned some bad vibes into my backpack," he stifled into genuine laughter during his recounting.

Isaac recalled the small cut on his abdomen from jumping the fence, stinging the entire day, to the phone call she had later received that night about his absence fourth, fifth, and sixth period classes.

"God, I thought we were such badasses. Actually, we kinda were. And now look at us."

Isaac chuckled. "Times were nicer. Funny. Random thing to bring up, too."

"Nice to take a stroll down memory lane some time."

Isaac nodded in acknowledgement, twirling his last tender over a lost appetite.

All he could focus on now was her. The woman from a past memory, tending to his cut. The woman that was his caretaker for years, even after his parents passed away. A woman without a name. For if she had a name, Isaac would be forced to face his past consequences.

'No,' Isaac thought. 'Not yet.'

* * *

He double-checked the map prior to tonight, confirming that no warehouse was marked there. This had to lead to something new.

The warehouse was located at a commerce building in The Bronx, now a dead zone. Isaac had visited this area in the past a few times, but never noticed the commerce area with all the buildings. Only one amongst the decayed architecture brimmed with dim lights.

Isaac approached the 10-story building, the echoes of chatter becoming prominent as he stepped closer. He climbed up a nearby escape ladder, eventually reaching the rooftop entrance. The upper floors were empty, while two voices echoed in a nearby stairway.

"This is it..." one voice said, "Your moment..."

"Not ready...I'm not...don't want..."

A boom shook the building. "Shut it..."

As Isaac tiptoed, one wrong step led him to plummeting

down 7 floors, surrounded by thugs adorning different gear on a hollowed decayed floor. More armored than the usual crowd. But Isaac prepared his stance, ready to fight. This was his therapy.

Precise strikes, weaving in and out of attacks depicted by the holograms of the HUD prediction software. He hurdled through one enemy after another, relenting into a combo flowing like an ocean.

A punch, kick, grapple into a throw, followed by a three-punch combo, connecting into a sweep, dodging, and countering, until one punch Isaac didn't register, then another.

The force prompted him to stumble back. His body's momentum regained balance and followed with harder counters.

No one ever caught a glance of the smile he sometimes flashed thanks to the helmet veiling his expression. There was something to admire about the seamlessness of the fight, dashed with the spice of rage and adrenaline when backed into a corner.

Isaac never saw himself as a pro at fighting. Just an animal fighting until his heart stopped.

———

The head honcho arrived. A tall jackass with a jackass scowl, wearing a white suit and make-up disguised as scars. It seemed like a feign attempt at some kind of 'Diablo' aesthetic.

Isaac had seen this scenario one too many times. Some thugs believed Diablo resurrected, others went along with the scenario because the illusion of power equated to more money.

He wondered. What would happen if two fake Diablos encountered each other? Isaac chuckled at the thought of two imposters flailing at each other like puppets.

As Isaac charged towards the Diablo poser, the life drained from his eyes, unable to keep steady as he fell limp to the floor. Blurs of dark tints and barren colors coagulated into a silhouette, then washed over his sight, before turning black.

* * *

Isaac awoke, his body stiffened by the aches of his accumulated bruises and cuts. His arms were held back, as were his legs, against a wooden chair. The rope pressed into his body, stiffening his breathing.

This situation brought back memories of the unsettling

time he was captured by Diablo, and tortured endlessly, month by month, in that white room, where time and space was lost to Isaac.

"I need to..." Isaac said in short raps of air, "I need to go, I need to leave...Not again, no"-

He shifted his gaze up, noticing a boy with lanky limbs and messy blonde hair. His grey Henley draped loosely over his torso, and black joggers hugged below his waistline, overlapping his yellow grime-covered sneakers.

Around his neck was a catholic cross wrapped in a thin, gold chain. Standing next to him was a man of similar stature, covered in hair besides his head, from his beard to the chest hair puffing out of his tank-top.

The short, bearded man grinned widely, wrapping his arm around the teen's shoulder, while the latter stared at Isaac with wide, shaky pupils. His body trembled, clearly sweating from the sweltering heat. The window from behind revealed moonlight, veiling most of their expression with shadows.

"Bryant..." the short man said, "This is it...everything belongs to us at the top here. You'll have all your drugs, you stop being a fucking thief, and I keep a roof over our heads. All we gotta do is kill everyone in this room..."

Isaac turned to his left, finding the other men he fought restrained in chairs, including the bootleg Diablo.

"DAVEY! What in THE FUCK are you doing?!" The faux Diablo yelled, struggling to lash out from his restraints.

"Now's the time I get what's coming to me. You may have messed with the right people up until this point, but now you'll think in hell over and over how you should've given me the master keys."

"FUCK YOU!"

Davey laughed. "Alright, Bryant. It's time to kill these bastards."

"I..." Bryant's thin limbs shook tremendously as much as his chattering teeth, revealing a tiny, imperfect middle gap. He continued, "I don't want to..."

Davey paused. The eyebrows of his forehead closed the gap in-between. His upper lip jagged upward. "Are you fucking serious? Do I have to repeat myself again? Listen, you're not safe anymore...

"You understand you go to jail, right? Several, several

years in jail. Trust me when I say sure, there's a free room, free food and all that shit, but the free shit ain't enough to outweigh all the shit you go through. Stop thinking like a fucking retard."

"But," Bryant's teeth chattered, "Why?"

"STOP ASKING WHY!" Davey screamed from the pits of his lungs, "YOU KILLED SOMEONE, AND NOW YOU'RE GONNA DO WHAT I SAY, AND KILL THEM!! KILL THEM NOW, BRYANT!"

Bryant raised his arm, pointing at the first man down the line. "I'm sorryI'm sorryI'm sorry..." Bryant muttered as his shaky fingers extended outward.

The man's nose began bleeding, followed by his head contorting off his neck joint. "STOP, STOP," the man shrieked.

"DO IT!!!", Davey shouted.

The man's eyeballs bulged out of his head. Instantly, chunks of his head split apart into shrapnel, flying across the entire room. A piece bounced off Isaac's helmet. It was too quick to tell specifically what part of his head it was.

Blood shot out of his neck like a fountain, leaving a

lifeless, headless body.

'Holy shit...' Isaac thought. He slowly zig-zagged his hands out of the rope restraints. With time running thin, he hastened his escape. Amidst the screams, all Isaac could focus on was the popping sounds.

Pop. Pop. Pop. Leading to the faux Diablo. He eliminated all essence of fright, and roared, "I'LL VISIT YOU IN HELL, DAVEY, YOU FUCKING CUCK!"

Then, another Pop.

"Last one, kid. Finish him off," said Davey.

Bryant's extended hand centered on Isaac's gaze. Isaac froze for a split second, wondering if this was how he would die, now re-aligning with all his recent memories leading to this point.

Isaac chose to not go down without a fight. He desperately acted to loosen his restraints. His determination persevered even as the vision of his HUD turned static.

Seconds passed. No symptoms overcame Isaac. Nothing to signify he was in pain or dying. Bryant shook harder, more viscerally. He released his tension and brought his extended hand to his face. "I can't kill him..." Bryant exasperated.

The static faded back to a normal display. The loosened restraints allowed Isaac to break free and charge at the duo, aiming for the window behind them. "Not my time to deal with this," Isaac remarked.

"For fuck's sake," Davey said while Bryant covered his face with his arms. Davey pulled out a pistol from his waist and fired three shots as Isaac.

Isaac dashed left and right in a zig-zag pattern, a bullet passing through his left shoulder. He bashed his injured shoulder into Bryant, using the momentum to throw the boy into his father. Isaac collided through the windowpane. Fragmented glass shards sunk into his body.

Looking back, Davey and Bryant didn't try to pursue Isaac. The escape resulted as a success.

* * *

Arriving at the entrance of his home with a deep wound, Isaac marched upstairs through the vast mansion. Off-balance from the loss of blood, he stumbled off the end of the stairway to the bathroom. He removed his helmet followed by his hoodie and bulletproof vest.

———

Lightheaded, hot flashes from the intensity of the bath-room lights stunned Isaac.

From the bottom cabinet, Isaac pulled out a bottle of alcohol, a thread and needle, and a metal detector. Laid out intricately, he started by scanning around his shoulder with the metal detector. No sounds of beeps, signifying he was safe from having any trace of shrapnel stuck in his wound.

He twisted off the cap from the bottle of alcohol and pushed through deafening screams as ounces of the liquid made contact.

Isaac remarked on the miniscule size of the wound. It could've been much worse. He looped the thread through the needle, readying for the suture.

With his off-hand, Isaac pinched the wound together. Next, carefully, just like in all the wiki-how's and amateur YouTube videos he watched, he poked through one side of the wound, and carried the threaded needle across. "90 degrees, 90 degrees," he repeated aloud. The amount of effort into this precision dragged the procedure on like if hours had passed.

Isaac sighed, the pain and pressure subsiding. He leaned back against the white porcelain wall.

His mind reflected on Bryant's mannerism. Limbs shaking, unable to keep composure. The stutters through his speech, unable to stare at the atrocities he was committing.

Isaac couldn't shake the imagery of all the trapped smugglers who screamed for their lives, white-eyed with nowhere to run. His mind wandered back to her. His gut dragged to the deepest pit, twisting around into knots, before dragging Isaac further into his own personal cubicle of hell..

III

BRYANT FIGUEROA

October 5, 2023 // 2:50 AM

Davey threw a punch, swift and sudden, against Bryant, sending him sliding across the shard-covered floor in the warehouse. Bryant's cheek swelled to a red welt as Davey stood above him.

Davey marched toward Bryant, while the latter struggled to desperately crawl away. Davey picked him up by the collars of his shirt. He yelled incoherent spit to his face. Bryant's fear swelled up into rage, but far from reaching a boiling point.

"WHAT THE HELL WAS THAT?!" Davey yelled spit onto Bryant's face.

"I don't know, I don't!" Bryant tripped over his words, thinking over why that masked man didn't die like the others. "The...the helmet! The helmet might have something to do with why."

Davey tilted his head back, locking his squint at Bryant. "What, like you have to see his face to make it blow up?"

"I don't know...I really don't know..."

"For fuck's sake," he shrugged, "You don't have an instruction manual with these powers?"

Bryant shook his head, so fast a patch of air escaped from his spinal joint.

Davey sighed. "Alright," Davey lifted his son up, "Up on your feet. Up, UP, or else more glass is gonna stick in ya."

Bryant found his footing, while the shards of glass sank deeper into his skin. "I think glass got stuck in my wrists..."

"Oh? Shame. Hospitals are something we have to avoid. Especially with this blood on us. Man, what a mess... You did a hell of a job on these people, kid, I'll give you that at least."

Davey walked over to his boss's corpse. He laughed, shouting, "Look at this!" The lower half of his bosses' head was still attached as he picked up the corpse by the back of the suit's collar, bobbing it up and down like a puppet.

"Boy, did I lose my marbles. I think I need an ibuprofen!" Davey cackled during his high-pitch mockery.

Bryant stared frozen, registering the intact torso and limbs spattered in red, followed by the pale neck, then the flesh-patch chin. Counting each tooth dangling off the corpses' lower jaw.

* * *

His vision blacked out. The sudden surge of cold water transported him back to his house, with his father leaning over him.

"Oh, now you're awake. You weigh a lot more than you look, kid," said Davey. "Pull it together."

"Wha...What happened?" The water washed away bits of the embedded glass shards from his limbs, trailing small crimson rivers down the drain.

"Yeah, you passed out! I'm going to bed, clean this trash up." Davey walked out, leaving Bryant in the tub. Bryant realized he was still in his clothes, now soaked and weighing him down. He wrapped his hand over the gold catholic cross worn around his neck.

Bryant wondered what his friends were up to now, studying abroad across the world. They decided to move

————

and study under prestige scholarships after all of them graduated 4 months ago, besides Josh. Bryant was left here in New Manhattan, where Josh opened his eyes to M.A.D. and the party life of New Manhattan.

Crowds brushed past him. They all focused their attention on Josh. Bryant was waiting for one person to start a conversation, to not dart a weird glance. Yet, Bryant didn't know how to behave properly.   His reactions were timed poorly, spending too much time thinking on what to say or do.

Bryant always knew about his father's job, finding his stash of M.A.D. in the worst hiding spots like cookie jars, unlocked drawers, and mattress crevices.

In the past 2 days, he finally built up the courage, like a cub confronting the lion's den, to steal it for the nightlife. When Bryant stole the stash and brought it to parties, it made him the highlight. Everyone began to surround Bryant.

These people, from obnoxious drunks to scantily clad women shrouded in flashes of neon lights, only beamed a smile, glowing from the blacklight, at Bryant and waltzed away after they got their dose. But all it took was one smile. One smile to ignite the euphoria. To share more than the glance and nod. It was the insane spark Bryant wanted.

M.A.D. only amplified the blissful emotions. Bit by bit, it overtook his train of thought. The nights he once enjoyed turned to chunks that only outlined the times he was happiest, like a burned film reel.

Bryant remembered the day Davey nearly caught him. His smile shattered. His mind warped to all the moments of Davey smacking him, provoking him to fight back, or when he neglected his son by not giving him meals for several days.

There were the nights his mom vanished, only to return the day after next. With every stranger, Bryant always wondered when the day would come that a stranger would enter, but without his mother or Davey.

That was the first meltdown. Everyone saw every angle of Bryant, some unsure of why he was acting this way, and some immediately knowing. One of those being Josh. Josh was the one to convince Bryant to stop using M.A.D. Bryant remembered Josh's words after he agreed to stop.

It'll only get worse if you spiral further. Stopping is the right choice.

<hr>

Back to the present day, Bryant was unable to think any more about his past nights. "God..." he mumbled, sinking his face into his soaked jeans, "How long do I have to suffer through this? Fuck..." His stealthy sobs were diffused by echoes against the tub's hollow surface.

Blue jays chirped outside, jolting Bryant awake. He stumbled out of the bathtub and shut off the running water. He switched off the light, revealing daylight from the outdoor window.

He sat through the entire night without realizing. Bryant exited the bathroom, leading into the ripped carpet halls and a table cluttered with Ziploc bags of random junk, newspapers, and dirtied Tupperware. One of the table's legs were supported by two bricks.

To his left, Bryant stood in front of a broken mirror nailed to the wall. The remaining shards piled up on the table directly underneath. Bryant's gaze wandered to the indented scars his knuckles left behind after breaking the mirror.

Next to the shards were envelopes. One of them an unopened letter from Sage Foundations: an internship Bryant applied for, but never decided to follow back on due to feeling too tired to focus. The first stage of his withdrawal.

<hr>

When the withdrawal happened, the mirror was one of the first things he broke. Also, one of the first times something shattered so instantaneous upon contact. The walls kept their foundation, the few people he fought in clubs stood their ground. Maybe he always held back, until the rage boiled over like a pot of overcooked pasta.

By the corner of the front door laid the family dog Mayer. A light brown dachshund, ribs exposed, laying by an empty silver bowl. "They forgot about you again…," said Bryant. While his dad was doing his daily routine of pretending to work, his mother disappeared to another business trip without a word.

At this point, it was 3 strangers living in a house together.

Bryant darted to the kitchen. He shuffled through the cabinets until he found the remaining third of dog food. Bryant shook the bag as he walked over to the bowl, sparking the dog back to life.

Mayer's tail wagged as he lunged up and scooped out chunks of the waterfall of pellets into his mouth. Bryant was pouring into the bowl.

"Alright Mayer, alright," Bryant chuckled. "Good boy."

———

                              * * *

Sunlight attacked Bryant's nocturnal eyes as he stepped
outside. 'What day was it?' he wondered, scratching around
his ashy eyelids. 'Saturday? Sunday? No, no, Wednesday
was yesterday. Thursday.'

This would mark his 2nd week in a row being absent
from school. He should make an appearance, he thought. At
least try to.

'How the hell could people have so many friends?' Bryant thought to himself passing through the crowded side-
walks and subways of social butterflies to arrive on campus. There had to have been a secret trick or technique.

A giant, open hall stretched down to a handful of class
auditoriums. He kept his gaze forward, refusing to turn
to the sides at risk of seeing his reflection on windows or
sleek surfaces.

Bryant turned towards the adjacent building to find his
reflection. A pale complexion, dried strands of dishev-
eled hair, wrinkled clothing, a face covered in blood. He
blinked, then seeing his face clean again, overtaken by the
dry cracks and dark circles.

The detail was never directly in Bryant's sights, nor did

anyone make note. But the blood stuck for the past day, flickering on and off, almost as if his brain was testing his conscience. The blood of all the people he killed. Invisible crimson oozing down his clothing from the crown of his head.

"Deep breaths, deep breaths. Think about some-thing else, what to eat for tonight. Maybe a sub, or even Funyuns. My lips are dry," Bryant said to himself, inhaling and exhaling, rinse, and repeat.

Bryant marched to class until he was stopped after a few feet by another man. A bit of scruff on him, wearing a fitted polo framing around buff pectorals and a slim abdominal stomach.

"Hey, Bryant," the man marched up to him, "Where is he?"

Bryant began to scratch his neck. "Uh...I'm confused. I don't know you. Who?"

"Where is he?" He shouted, attracting attention. "My boyfriend. He was with you. Come on, you guys are friends! I know he was smoking with you, that was the last time I got his text, 3 days ago."

'Fuck. Is this Josh's boyfriend?' Bryant thought, shaky

and stuttering. Bryant never met Josh's partner; let alone did he ever know that Josh had one to begin with due to Josh's single lifestyle on the dance floor.

Maybe it was a fluke, a misunderstanding. Bryant zig-zagged his eyes to the reflection, then the man's polo, then to the floor. "I genuinely don't know you, or who you're talking about…I'm not trying to be rude; I swear."

"Josh," the man replied, "You're friends with him. I've seen photos of you two together."

"Ah…Ah, no," Bryant's head ignited, triggering the night from 3 days ago. After the panic attack, the moment of his withdrawal, after his father took back his entire stash upon discovery. After Bryant punched the mirror and walked 3 blocks until Josh came to pick him up.

Bryant's lungs were ready to shoot out of his chest from overabundant hyperventilation. All the while Josh's voice, strung in echoes, itched the back of Bryant's head.

'I need it. I need it. Just give me something. I'm dying,' were his words. Josh's words were to take a deep breath. This wasn't Bryant. Bryant was better than this.

'Josh didn't comprehend shit,' Bryant recalled. He recalled the deafening pitch burning into his ear drums.

———

Traffic disappeared. Cars honking vanished. The chirps of birds and insects were all but faded. He had to scream. He screamed for help, despite being sure no one listened.

Bryant emerged back to the reality of now. "Who...who are you?"

"Are you fucking with me right now, Bryant? It's Chris. Josh's boyfriend. We may not hang out a lot but we hung out a few times. What the..." Chris squinted his eyes, leaning closer into Bryant.

He was examining Bryant's current vulnerability, the anxiety pinging around in Bryant's shaken widened stare, shifted down at the uneven cobblestone slabs.

"I'm...sorry..." Bryant lied. That's the same thing he said to Josh. Josh fought back against him. Josh said Bryant needed help. More M.A.D. wasn't the solution. He said Bryant should seek rehab to work himself out. Tears and sobs cracked through the pitches of Josh's baritone voice.

"Bryant..." said Chris, "Why are you sorry? You're hiding something. This is gonna lead into serious trouble if you don't tell me. I'm not afraid to beat the shit out of you if something happened to Josh."

"I... I didn't mean to...," said Bryant. The same thing he

said after he yelled at Josh, prompting the latter's head to combust. The wet blood laid bare on Bryant's vulnerable skin. The most notable detail was the brain matter being damp, sticking to Bryan's skin and hair.

Eventually the whole event registered to Bryant's head: those pieces on him were Josh's scattered remains.

Bryant screamed, the entire drive back to his house, hysterically running inside to ask his father for help. Of all the people, that was Bryant's first mistake.

Chris balled his left hand into a fist, striking Bryant's gut. "WHERE IS HE?! TELL ME BRYANT!"

"I... I JUST WANTED SOME MORE! THAT'S ALL!! SHUT UP, SHUT UP!!!" Bryant extended his arms at Chris, forcing the latter to his knees.

"I...my body..."

Veins pulsated around Bryant's arms, as he pummeled Chris continuously, colliding against bones that turned brittle, cracking upon each impact. Bryant stopped when he realized Chris became unresponsive.

No stiffening, no squirming, nor a grunting sound. "I... I'm sorry," said Bryant, "I'm so sorry...Josh is dead. I killed him. I killed Josh... I'm sorry." Bryant ran off the campus grounds, narrowing into a trance of tunnel vision.

* * *

Returning home, Bryant hid in his bedroom until the sun set into the evening. 5 bodies. Was it 5? Regardless, 5 bodies were 5 too many on Bryant's conscious. He couldn't handle it anymore. He was ready to split. Someone, any-one, needed to take Bryant out of this nightmare before he exploded.

The noise from outside signified the return of his father. His trademark Timberland boots stomped against the carpet to remove any trace of dirt and debris from the soles.

"Bryant. Bryant!" Davey stomped through the halls outside. "Get ready soon. We got plans." Bryant remained unresponsive. Davey slammed the door open. "Hey! You answer me when I yell for you."

"Didn't hear you," Bryant replied lowly.

"Oh, bullshit, look at the size of this house! We ain't in-vested in thick walls either."

Bryant struggled to find out how to adapt to tonight. His dad wasn't going to take no for an answer, nor an excuse like him being sick. Davey remained on his toes when it came to his son, ever since being exposed to the drug theft.

Then, he recalled that man from last night. The man with the black helmet. Fully black, unable to see a human face.

That man, between the mask and the face behind it. Bryant depicted them as two separate people. So, he imagined. That's what he needed. "Dad..." Bryant said. "I need a favor."

"What do you want?"

"Can I wear a mask? I need a mask."

"Why do you need a mask?"

"I can't..." Bryant couldn't find the proper words to rationalize with his father. "I just...I need one, please."

"Buddy, let me level with you," Davey sat down on Bryant's bed. He patted Bryant's shoulder, prompting an impulsive twitch from Bryant. "I know you've been going through a lot. This is…a lot. And you've been doing a lot of rebellious dumb shit prior to this, too. But where I'm going, where we're going, it's nowhere but the top. All the money and power."

'I don't want any of that,' Bryant thought, 'I just want peace.' Instead, he nodded, and replied, "I need a mask."

Davey shook his head, then chuckled, "Y'kno what, I got something." Davey walked out of the room, the stomps moving to the kitchen, slamming open some drawers, until the stomps followed back to Bryant's room.

Davey planted a brown paper bag against his chest. Something ordinary, brown, slightly torn and blotched with stains near the top ridges. "All yours, buddy," Davey said with a snide grin.

Bryant carved one hole out of the bag as an eye socket. He slid the mask over his face, hyperventilating, afraid of the darkness.

Limbs trembled as memories emerged of all the killings, all the phantom blood and wetness that he couldn't wash off.

After a few seconds, there was no longer terror. This darkness, with the small hole acting as a lens to the outside world, was an environment Bryant felt calm. He imagined himself submerged in the dark.

———

The phantom blood wasn't an element to alienate. His hyperventilation calmed to a rhythmic meditation, still submerged. Bryant wouldn't need to worry about these troubles. Because this new face wasn't Bryant.

He clasped his hands around his gold necklace and chanted a prayer.

This wasn't him, as Josh said. Bryant could rest.

IV

Isaac Sage

October 5, 2023 // 3:10 PM

He stood by his window, gazing outside with a bag of ice braced against his head. Dots of people glided in and out, almost never bumping into each other. Truthfully, the last thing Isaac wanted to do today was file papers. He couldn't stop thinking about that kid Bryant, and his strange power.

And he couldn't stop thinking where he was now. Causing chaos? Killing more people? The thoughts worried Isaac. But he was unsure of where the worry stemmed from.

Someone cleared their throat, catching Isaac's attention. Isaac turned to find Mr. Gallagher. His oval, wrinkled head glistened against the light, contrasting against the dark purple turtleneck he wore, covering most of his lean stature.

A surprise, as Isaac hadn't seen him in months. "Isaac," Mr. Gallagher spoke, "Good to see you."

"Mr. Gallagher, good afternoon. How are you?" Isaac asked.

"Good, thank you. I'd been meaning to drop by in the past few months. Supervisors have been telling me..." A pause. It was leading to either something wonderful or something very, very bad.

"Your work has been keen," Mr. Gallagher continued. "Spot-on, even. Your demeanor, however, has been...what's the right word...isolating, yes. That's the word. Your isolated behavior's been bringing down the morale a bit."

"I apologize. My own headspace can distract me often." Mr. Gallagher kept a firm, neutral expression. Isaac's nerves prompted him to explain further. "Y'kno, its"-

"No need," Gallagher interjected, "I understand. Try to be positive soon. Just...keep fighting. If you need someone to talk to, you have us."

'Keep fighting. Keep fighting.' Isaac pondered further on his past recent actions. Through all the fighting and time spent on raiding warehouses…was this vendetta worth

———

anything? Was it important to stop Bryant? Or should he do nothing at all?

'No,' Isaac thought. 'This, all of this, had to be worth something.' Every sacrifice had to lead to something good. This new enemy was just another roadblock that Isaac was forced to overcome.

"Thank you for the kind sentiments," Isaac said. "I'll do my best to improve." He suddenly reminisced on his parents hard-working ethics. It was what made Sage Foundations to the icon it was now, and decades ago.

"Maybe I can be included in the business practices? As a shadow?" Isaac asked.

Mr. Gallagher reacted with a raised brow. He smiled. "I see that soft gleam of your father's eyes. And that determined brow…Gemma always made that expression impulsively. Why not?"

Gallagher placed his hand on Isaac's shoulder. "But first, start coming to work on time consistently," he smiled. "How's that sound?"

Red-faced, Isaac nodded. "Yes, sir."

* * *

———

Concluding his shift, Isaac exited the Sage building, tossing the bag of melted ice into the closest bin. Charcoal swept through the city air, igniting his hunger. A mix of meat, ketchup, mustard, and warm bread emanated from a small stand by the corner.

Isaac headed to the stand and ordered one hot dog, handed to him in wrapped foil. Warm to the touch. Soothing like the bag of ice against his head.

He proceeded down the block, getting into a subway. Throughout the ride, he made sure to eat his hot dog slowly enough to savor the meal, the hot sensation warming his palm.

Not far from home, he received a call from Todd.

"Hey man," Todd said, "How was your day?"

"I've had better days," said Isaac. "Headed home early."

"Oh, awesome. That makes me more confident in what I'm about to ask next. Let's have a beer tonight, yeah? I need to break my day-to-day pace."

"Really?" Isaac said, shocked to be seeing Todd two days in a row. He'd grown so accustomed to the isolation that his immediate reaction was to feign an excuse, especially since tonight was to pursue Bryant and Davey.

But it was clear that cabin fever was building up to a breaking point. "Let's do it," Isaac said.

"Cool, man. Talk about the easiest time to arrange something!" said Todd, "I'll see you later tonight."

"Looking forward to it. Take care." Isaac hung up, now arriving at the mansion, vast and empty like before. His footsteps being the only ambience. He balled up the foil and tossed it away after finishing his hot dog.

Choosing to pursue the threat. Choosing to see Todd tonight. The traumatic memories slowly forming back. Isaac decided to visit her out in the backyard with this free time.

Her burial was there. The body buried so far deep into the dirt and placed far enough out into the open greenery behind Isaac's mansion. Hidden, with no tombstone. Only flowers and a mound of dirt.

"Hey again," said Isaac. "I'm sorry I didn't bring flowers this time. Big thing tonight. You would've stopped me at this point if you were still here." The wind chilled the base of his neck, raising goosebumps.

He remembered a lot of her, from her kindness to her willingness to help. A pit dug open in his heart, telling him he committed something awful. For the first time, he recognized his uncertainty on the path he was fated to take.

The blades of grass swayed back and forth. Nothing but himself, her and the vast plane of land. The surroundings ranged so different from the cityscape, like a chunk of land was taken from the middle of the purest landscape, untouched by any human, and transported to Isaac's backyard.

He kneeled by the grave, shutting down his mind for some time. The sun's intense heat vanished. His pores dried up. Even the wind stopped speaking. This moment was rare for Isaac, always surrounded by sounds buzzing in his head, keeping him either anxious or alert.

After his short reprieve, Isaac headed back inside, preparing to gear up. Boots, pants, vest, hoodie. And finally, the helmet. He stared at his reflection through the helmet. A welded scar down the middle, from his fight with Diablo.

If only, Isaac wondered, if only this face held on to the memories he faced in all those tragedies, all those deaths. Someone to carry the burden of it all. After all the tragedy removed, who would Isaac Sage be, if not nothing but a dull moniker for his tragic memories?

Everyone saw the mask as another face. But Isaac Sage knew, without a doubt, he and this other face were the same, two shades of the same palette. There was no escaping it.

The sun set, giving Isaac the opportunity to make his way across the cityscape of New Manhattan, onward to the Bronx district.

* * *

Arriving at the building, now cast in yellow lights instead of the natural ice-blue moonlight. Isaac checked the rooftop once more. No traps installed. No wires or sensors raised alarms from the HUD of his helmet. Regardless, Isaac remained cautious.

The foundation of the stairs held its ground, sturdy enough with each creeping step Isaac took. Frighteningly, the walls swayed with a subtle lateral movement. Isaac was unsure how long the building would stay intact.

He headed down to the fourth floor, where a large gap was now unearthed in the center. Crouched, he crawled along to the edge, peering down at what laid below.

A crowd of smugglers, about 10 or 15, surrounded Davey and Bryant. Some wielding firearms, some standing with

their arms folded. Their uniforms consisted of loose clothing of mismatched colors.

Davey wore a brown leather jacket, while Bryant wore
the same clothes from the other night. This time his face
was covered with a brown paper bag.

"Wait, so," one of the smugglers said, "The boss is
dead? You killed the boss?"

"No, I didn't. He did," Davey pointed over to Bryant.
"Got the body and everything too, if you're into the gory
details."

"Nah man. This is fucked. You should bury him and go
somewhere else. Higher-ups are gonna cap your ass."

Many of the others surrounding the vocal smuggler
nodded their heads in agreement.

"What are you saying?" Davey retorted. "Think you
should choose your words more wisely?"

"If I could be any wiser, Davey, I'd tell you to take
your head out of your ass and realize ya killed our source
of income. Now you expect to understand the business and
bring the same money?"

"I'm not an idiot."

The smuggler scoffed. "Yeah. You fucked us over, Davey. All because you were being a punk bitch."

Davey stifled, taking a deep breath. He shifted his eyes to the floor. "Do it," he commanded.

Bryant raised his arm at the smuggler, smooth like a well-oiled wheel.

And just like that, Pop. A fountain of blood sprayed out, and the smuggler's body fell to the floor, headless.

The other armed men pointed their weapons at Davey and Bryant. Bryant rotated his arm around the room, transforming the floor into a sea of headless corpses and a bath of crimson red. Soon, many of them began retreating away, trying to escape the damage.

Isaac leapt down, landing on top of Bryant, followed by a swift hook across his paper-covered face. Isaac approached Davey.

"You think you can take ME down, freak?" Davey backed away from Isaac, shuffling through his pockets, "As soon as I find this pistol, you're dead..."

"Oh, fuck off!" Isaac launched a swift, hard straight punch square into Davey's face. He gestured to the remaining smugglers alive. "The rest of you, GO!" Their stampedes provoked the building to shake severely. Isaac couldn't pinpoint how much longer this building would stand.

"Hey..." A voice signaled to Isaac.

Isaac groaned. "Not now, ghost voice," he turned, blocking Bryant's forearm strike by a sliver of an inch. Isaac's left arm began to swell up.

"Back off. Now." The voice connected with Bryant's hunched-over stature.

Isaac shook his head, responding with another hook to Bryant's face. Bryant swiftly went back into an offensive stance. His unfazed reaction was odd. In fact, the punch lacked Isaac's usual power.

Isaac's eyes grew heavier, his limbs heavier, and his breathing less steady. The HUD sounded off the alarms for Bryant's predicted results.

The best Isaac could do at his current energy level was block. He defended against half of the blows, taking the other half head-on. Each of Bryant's hits were equal to 10 consecutive punches from a pro boxer, or even a superhuman.

<hr>

Bryant's upper torso leaned backward, pulling back his lanky arms, and with a gigantic ground-shaking roar, slammed down Isaac with an overhand hook. The ground shook violently, enough for the floor beneath them to break and send them falling to the floor below.

Isaac's energy depleted, while Bryant was multiplying his output. As the former staggered, drenched in blood pouring from above, Bryant approached him with his open palm pointed at Isaac's face. The HUD accumulated in static amidst the two at a standstill.

"It... It won't work!" said Bryant. "Why won't it work?!?"

He loosened his arm, and in seconds the static faded. Isaac's natural energy returned. The static occurred the other night, Isaac deduced. It worked with no hesitation on the others. But he, the only one with a helmet...

Waves. The helmet produced electromagnetic waves. That was Bryant's weakness. He had to raise the output on his electro gloves to highlight Bryant's weakness. Isaac pondered the best opening for his attack to do this.

Isaac lashed out, testing with his depleting energy, the gloves tuned at the highest output. Bryant retracted both his arms, preparing for another wild flail. His torso was now wide open.

The closer he approached Bryant, the longer the waves were resonating. Isaac's energy was returning.

At the last inch, Isaac stretched his fist out into an open palm, and slammed it against Bryant's chest. The blast fired from the glove, forcing Bryant's whole body to convulse in shock, followed by a second concussive energy propelling Bryant's body across the room. Isaac ran over to Bryant, ready to strike the final blow to confirm the teen was unconscious.

Isaac swiped the paper bag off Bryant's head. Isaac's fist raised above his head, ready to strike down with 100% of his force.

At the sight of Bryant's widened eyes, trembling pupils, and aghast expression, Isaac froze. It brought a flash of her. Her, in those final moments before Isaac killed her, in his drug-fueled insanity. The awful thing he committed returned to fruition.

"What...what happened?" Bryant shouted. "I...I..."

Isaac relaxed his muscle. "You're fine," he said calmly, "You should rest." Bryant was only a puppet. The real threat to handle was...

Bang. A gunshot fired from behind, grazing Isaac's hoodie. "Found my gun," Davey said. "That was a warning shot."

Isaac raised his hands up. "I give."

"No shit, you give," Davey said, "I'm gonna have Bryant here pummel the shit out of you..."

"I've only met you twice, and I'm not surprised," Isaac shrugged, "Can't do a thing for yourself."

Davey laughed, "Really?" He forced Isaac to turn around. He pressed the barrel of the gun against Isaac's helmet. The load of the bullet into the gun's chamber echoed. Static softly veiled around the edges of his HUD. Isaac closed his eyes. All he could think about was her.

Kara.

"I bet this helmet ain't bulletproof," Davey smiled.

Then...

Pop. The gun clanged against the damp floor. Isaac opened his eyes to a headless Davey swaying back and forth lifelessly. Isaac turned to Bryant, one hand extended out towards his father's corpse, trembling. "He...he wouldn't have stopped," Bryant said. "He wouldn't have, right?"

Isaac shook his head. 'I'm sorry' is what he wanted to say. But, in his mind, where would that lead to, and who would it save? Instead, he said, "Let's leave. This build-ing's not safe."

By the time Isaac and Bryant walked downstairs and exited the building, all the other smugglers had left the blackout zone. They walked further, with only the cres-cent-shaped moon above lighting their path.

They proceeded through the alleyways and past all the intersections, until Bryant stopped. "Would you sit with me?" Bryant asked. "I feel sick...Unless you don't want to."

"Not at all. I'm fine with that."

The two sat down on the sidewalk. Roots protruded out of the concrete, making the seat uneven in height.

"I killed a lot of people. I didn't mean to. Are you gon-na send me to the police?"

"No. Not an altruistic person myself." Isaac kept his eyes fixed to the concrete.

"I think you're a hero. You do right things. You stopped me. You tried stopping my dad, and all those other people. Those were all bad people, I think. They killed for fun."

"You killed because you were forced to."

"You knew that?"

"I could tell from your face. Y'kno, when the mask wasn't on. You weren't enjoying any of that," Isaac turned to Bryant, "You're a good kid, Bryant. You got potential to bring positive change."

"Would you be able to live with killing so much? Like, live freely?"

"I don't know," Isaac said, thinking about his own death count. Including Kara. Especially Kara. "I really don't know if that's for me."

He turned to Bryant. The teen was affixed at his gold necklace. "I'm Catholic, y'kno? Or at least I try to be. I don't go to church since my parents gave up early on. I felt there was a purpose, still. That He would lead me to the right path."

"I'm sure He is. This is all a part of the path you have to take. Just do your part to have that better future."

Bryant shook his head, "The more I think about it, the more I feel it's too late."

"You're still going through the shock of this all, Bryant. You...need time to process."

"How would you know?"

"PTSD. I went through therapy for that, so I would say my sources are legitimate."

"I can't..." Bryant sunk his face into his knees. He sobbed, "I can't do this to my mom. I killed my dad. I KILLED MY DAD!"

Isaac reflected on the partial memories he remembered of the night Kara died. The hysterical grief that strickened through his body the day after was crystal-clear. Isaac chose to remain silent.

"So why not?" Bryant continued.

"Why not what?"

"Why can't you kill me? Come on. I'm just an ant. No one will notice. I'm an ant. Less significant than that, even."

"Bryant, don't say stuff like that. I'm not gonna kill

you, but I'm gonna punch you senselessly if you don't stop spouting that."

"How am I gonna live? How? I'm a threat. I killed my friend by accident. His boyfriend fucking knows because I told him, I cracked earlier today. I can't go back... I already imagine the look on his face. On yours too. Behind that helmet, you're losing pity for me."

A boom echoed from a few miles away, sweeping the ground level with a mist of debris. Pigments stuck to Bryant's light hair.

Isaac's heart skipped a beat. A split-second trace of air that was unable to be inhaled. A spark ignited. Behind the mask, he scowled at Bryant, who gleamed a small smirk. Bryant was counting the seconds, waiting for Isaac to deliver the killing blow.

Was it too late for both?

Isaac exhaled shakily, shoulders tensing up. His fingers gripped around the gravel flooring. "Don't..." Isaac whimpered.

Bryant turned to Isaac and smiled. "You're a killer. You can live with that. I don't have that in me. It's alright."

This whole time he'd been fighting the identity of being a killer, running away from it.   Isaac wrapped both his hands around Bryant's neck.

Shocks sparked out of the gloves, leaving burn marks. Smoke exhumed from the point of impact. Bryant's neck was so frail that the bones protruded close to the superficial skin. It was so easy.

No one had been able to say it to his face until now. And how dare they, Isaac thought. Bryant stifled for air. Grey static formed around Isaac's vision.

Alone, bearing the pain once more with no one else to lean on. 'I don't know if I can do this anymore,' Isaac thought, reflecting on this cycle continuing endlessly. 'Can I do this on my own?'

Isaac roared. Nothing except the static's shrill reverberated back to his eardrums.

V

TODD ANDERSON

October 6, 2023 // 2:32 AM

Auburn lights kept the bar glowing with warmth, shining through its mosaic chandeliers hung throughout the locale. Todd sat by the bar top, spinning around an empty clear glass, equal in diameter to the palm of his hand. He sighed, turning to the entry door.

"Hey, buddy," said the bartender. "Bar's gonna close in 30 minutes. You want anything besides a water?"

"Um. Yeah, sure. Could I have a gin and tonic? Hold the lime," said Todd.

The bartender nodded, and proceeded to grab a new, highball glass, filling it with three ice cubes. He meticulously added the gin followed by tonic water with a gentle stir. "You sure you don't want lime?"

———

"Don't worry about it. I was waiting for someone but let me drink this and be out of your way."

"Take your time. Cheers."

Todd turned to the entry door once more. Nothing. He waited in hopes Isaac would show up. With every passing minute, his tensions of anger prolonged further. Instead of Isaac wasting his time, he could be spending it working on one of his projects. Perfecting his craft to make the life he wants.

But truth be told, Todd refused to spend another night in his thoughts. Even if they were free of the voices, something compelled him to sink into his feelings of aggression. The vision of black tar clung in his mind.

The door swung open. A silhouette of lean, athletic stature. The silhouette moved into the light, revealing it as Isaac. He walked in, wearing a ¾ sleeve Henley, and a pair of denim jeans.

"Damn man," said Todd, "Your guns are looking weak."

"Haven't they always?" Isaac sat on the empty barstool beside Todd. "I'm sorry I got here so late. You already know..."

"Ah, yep. Stuff I pretend to comprehend that I don't comprehend."

Isaac sighed, "Yep. How've you been?"

"Still tired. I'm so done with this whole studying shit."

"I imagine."

"And you?"

"Hanging in there." Isaac raised his hand and called out to the bartender. "You still serving, boss?"

"I can squeeze you in," said the bartender. "You paying cash?"

"Yeah. Whiskey, on the rocks."

"You got it."

Isaac turned back to Todd. "What time do they close in this place?"

"30 minutes or so."

"Jesus. Well, we can take this conversation outside, if need be," Isaac pointed his index finger at Todd's glass. "You and your damn gin and tonic, I don't get it."

———

Todd heard it all before from Isaac. He rolled back his eyes and replied, "Oh, here we go again with your hatred for gin and tonic"-

"WITHOUT limes, man. You're basically making your tongue suffer." The bartender slid the glass over to Isaac. Isaac laid down a $20 bill. "Thanks."

"Look at you, acting scruff with your whiskey. Do you pay respects to your beard now before you take a sip?"

"Fuck off," Isaac paused before taking a sip from his glass. "That doesn't even make sense."

Todd burst laughing. "You just did it!"

Isaac shook his head, "Now I remember why I don't hang out with you anymore," he said dryly.

"Ouch."

"I'm kidding, I'm kidding."

"At least you were able to grow something. The most I got were three baby hairs on my chin. Their names were Paul, Ted, and Chet."

"Were?"

"Gone too soon..." A beat of silence. Todd turned to

Isaac, noticing his mouth puffed like a blowfish, stifling back his swig of whiskey. Todd burst out laughing again. Followed by Isaac choking down his drink, clearing his throat while controlling his laughter.

In the amount of time passed, a lot changed in each other's circumstances. Yet here they sat in the bar after being disconnected for the past 6 months and the year before that. To Todd, it reminded him of two people that had remembered they were brothers-in-arms. Todd missed this greatly.

When the laughter settled, Isaac responded. "This is nice, getting to hang out for the past 2 days. I've been out of it for some time."

"Yeah. Same here. Reminds me of the good times."

Isaac smiled in reciprocation, affixed to his glass. The amber pool remained steady, while the ice slowly lost its solidity.

Todd continued, "Have you heard from anyone at campus? Rose?"

"No, not anyone, especially Rose. Things didn't go well between us if you recall. I hope she's fine."

"Me too."

Another beat of silence. The same grim expression laid bare on Isaac's face. With all the wrinkles from his soured, melancholy face, one would think he instantly aged 10 years. The mosaic lights shut down, leaving only the light above the two.

"5 minutes, fellas," said the bartender.

"Listen, Todd..." Isaac sighed. "I gotta level myself with you. And, in that way, to finally come clean."

"What's up?" Todd leaned in, attentive while Isaac rubbed his eyes, now reddened and irritated.

"I...." Isaac broke into a chuckle. "Fuck. I don't know where to start. None of it makes sense even though I've been having it make sense for me all this time."

"Lay it on me." Nothing came of it. Isaac kept silent. His eyes darted to the left, then right, then to the table, while one hand-spun the glass of watered-down whiskey. "We're literally in a bar with no one around if that's the is-sue. I think we're fine."

He stopped spinning the glass, and locked eyes on Todd. "I've been raiding warehouses where M.A.D is being smuggled."

Todd blinked. He blinked again, and again, registering what Isaac just said. He stifled a chuckle and replied, "What do you mean, raiding? How?"

"I... I gear up. I have a map with locations of different operating warehouses circled, I pick one, go and check to verify. If not, then on to the next one. If it is, well..." Isaac paused.

Todd nodded, raising his eyebrows. "Well? I'm not gonna finish your sentence."

"I plan. I plan what to do, what's their weak points. Then, I attack. Beat them unconscious. I drag their bodies to a safe area. Then I set the warehouse on fire."

Todd recalled small stories being covered on the news, but never made note of it, it being nothing more than that. They made their cycles through internet forums and subreddits, with news just catching wind of it.

But to have his friend being the one behind those attacks, it left him speechless. He was mixed with shock and anger. "Shit..." Todd said.

"Alright," said the bartender, "Time to get out."

The duo walked out the door leading into the alleyway.

———

Todd began registering all the times Isaac excused his absence. All the lines and excuses he spilled to Todd.

Todd was angry at that moment, sure, but he believed every word of it. That was what made him more infuriated. He tried his best to rationalize with Isaac's logic. "So, all those times you were out of school..." Todd asked without looking Isaac in the eye. "All those times you were MIA... that was because?"

"Yeah," Isaac said.

"Yeah," Todd scoffed. "Yeah. Yeah."

"You alright?"

"Yeah, are you? I just don't understand why you couldn't tell me."

"Come on, Todd. Even I knew what I was doing was outrageous."

"So why were you doing it? Is it contract work for Sage Foundation? Re-capturing resources?"

"No. I found the guy who killed my parents. The one that blew up the building 16 years ago."

More exposition that Todd wasn't expecting. "What?"

"He was connected to the warehouses. I went through so many people. I fought tooth and nail. I trained so much to find the man and bring justice and closure, leave everything related in the past. Let my parents' rest."

"Jesus, Isaac. Why didn't you tell me? Why?"

"Because...your train of logic didn't align with mine. It seemed dumber than mine if I'm going to be honest now."

Todd paused. 'Dumber?' he thought. His breath shook. Isaac's stare remained steadfast. For a split-second, Todd swore his neutral grin broke into a conniving smirk. He coiled back his right arm and swung his momentum against Isaac's face.

"ARE YOU FUCKING KIDDING ME?!" Todd shouted with no mind to the public nearby, "Isaac, I'm your only friend, I care about the shit you go through!" He flexed his right hand, forgetting it was still injured.

"I know that…" Isaac groaned. "I've been alone for the past 6 fucking months, of course I know that."

"Whatever. I was always wondering what the hell you were dealing with, ME! I figured you had to focus on yourself, but not like this. And you're the one calling my logic dumber"-

Suddenly, Todd was sent flying against the opposite wall of the alleyway. His right cheek collided with the brick, pushing his momentum towards the adjacent trash can, shedding blood upon contact. His left cheek stung from the brute, instant force behind Isaac's fist.

Isaac stood over Todd while Todd kept track of him from the corner of his eye.

"YOU said it," Isaac spat, "YOU said it out of thin air, unprompted, plain and simple. 'It's pointless. A fairy tale ending that never happens. There're better things to pursue in life.' YOU DIDN'T KNOW!"

"I know well enough that revenge isn't the answer," Todd coughed, slowly recovering. "If there's one thing I hate, it's that kind of selfish attitude that you're trying to get something done for your gain alone. The last thought was how taking down this guy would help others right?"

Isaac didn't respond.

"Right?!" Todd yelled. "But it doesn't matter. Whatever the cost, yeah? Just sacrifice your whole life in this ditch?"

Isaac looked up to the skies, exhaling through his nose. "To be in a building erupting with fire and smoke, watching your parents go in one after the other. To think about that same thing, and to think about being helpless for 15 years. I wished I could've met that killer earlier; I wish he was caught so that I'd sleep well knowing my parents got the justice they deserved. They didn't. It was wiped under the rug as a freak accident."

Todd wanted to find something good-hearted from his friend's decisions. But the logic wasn't aligning. "How could you know?"

"What?"

"You mean to tell me you knew a killer existed this whole time? With no empirical evidence? Not one leak?"

"That doesn't matter. My gut feeling was right, and it led to it being right. He said it to my face, Todd. My parents were gone from this planet by someone's hand, someone that lived in this city. So how..." Isaac's speech stuttered momentarily, "How could I face anybody, knowing what I did, what I have to live with now..."

Todd lifted himself up with the brick wall. "Isaac...what did you do?" Isaac fell to his knees, then buckling to his hands. "You said you beat people to a pulp...but?"

"I didn't mean to...I only wanted to kill him," Isaac

wrapped his hands over the back of his head, deeply exhaling. "I had blackouts. They continued occurring. That led to killing one, and another, and another. Not double digits. I hope not. Some of them probably had families. I try not to think about it since it eats me alive, but I do think about it. I have to live with that now."

His friend was broken, falling apart in front of him. While Todd still couldn't comprehend his insane logic, he was at least able to rationalize his approach. A friend had to help that way. He knew Isaac wasn't insane. Todd laid his hand on Isaac's back. "Accidents is one thing, Isaac, but to constantly black out and pulling those nights...You gotta stop."

"I can't. No, I can't...not until I find the solution."

"What answer is that?"

With every utterance of a word, Isaac wiped away the sobs, regaining some composure. His speech reverberated a scratched tone but remained coherent. "There's a solution that must make me feel at peace. To stop waking up with all this contempt.

Isaac clawed against the dirt, covered in rancid odors and beer-glass fragments. "It never vanished after that killer died. His death was so... instant. I wanted him to suffer. But the others...they suffered more. It's not fair...It's not fair."

Maybe it was a necessity beyond one's comprehension. Because from all the anger Todd harbored against his current life, he could find himself in Isaac's shoes.

Todd pondered on Isaac's dilemma more. Maybe, if the roles were switched, Todd would go down the same path Isaac had chosen.

"May God rest their souls, but," Todd replied, "maybe they died so you can push forward. So that you can achieve your peace."

Isaac turned to Todd with hollowed eyes. "Todd...they didn't deserve it. I'm not the center of the spotlight either. People shouldn't be dying on my behalf."

"Yeah, you're not, obviously. You don't know what those guys did before you met them. To be honest, you probably never will. Yeah, you couldn't accept the fate of just leaving things to rest. But now, you've done it. I think it's pointless to endlessly grieve over something set in stone. In a way, you must live for them. That's how you make it up."

The tension in Isaac's body released. He slowly rose. Todd extended his hand, helping him up. A storm of fire still stirred from within "Thank you...I don't know if I deserve it, but"-

"I'll stop you there. You don't deserve a parade of applause, you're right about that. But you deserve to move forward." Todd then pulled Isaac in by the shoulder. "Swear to me you're not gonna throw your life away. You try to make any kind of move like that, then I'm out. And you're done as well."

Isaac shifted down. He took a moment to form his response. He closed his eyes and nodded. "I swear."

"Listen. Your secret's safe with me. Let me help you find that solution you're looking for. Maybe something else will find you closure. Or shutting down these operations will bring closure, since it is your parent's work and all. Or something else. You'll find a way, you're smart. Kind of."

Isaac scratched his head and leaned against the wall. His eyes glossed to the ground then back at Todd. "You're right...I mean, we'll see. How are you gonna help me?"

"I got some tricks up my sleeve. This master's degree won't be going to waste."

Isaac smiled. "Man, I've been shit to you. I'm sorry."

"Don't worry about it. You're paying for my beers and lunch from here on out. Once every week, we meet up. In other words, we go beyond this and get you out of this rut asap."

Isaac reached his hand out. "Deal..." Todd accepted, shaking Isaac's hand. A brotherhood finally rekindled, and, in Todd's hopes, for the better. "You gonna be alright getting home?"

"I should be asking that about you," Todd replied.

"I'll be fine."

"Better?"

"My chest feels lighter. Feeling better enough to follow your advice. For once."

Todd chuckled. "That's good thinking. I better not find you beating yourself up anymore."

Isaac nodded. The smile subtly faded. He turned around, without looking Todd in the eye, and marched out of the alleyway. "I'll try my best. See you."

"Don't be a stranger again," Todd waved. He looked up

at the sky. Blank, voidness. The streetlights of the city were cast against the black concrete, while the remaining lights in the buildings occupying New Manhattan began to leave the dark lit by whatever the moonlight was able to reach.

The murmuring of incoherent echoes re-emerged, scrambling Todd's head. A degree of teeth-gritting pain escalating to the point of his limbs locking up.

It had to be the adrenaline talking. All he needed to do was calm down. All they needed to do was remain vigilant. 'We all have to do our best,' He walked out the alleyway with gritted teeth. 'It's all we can do.'

EPILOGUE

Isaac Sage

October 6, 2023 // 4:28 AM

Isaac arrived home, immediately sweeping through the mansion, out the backdoor, and marching across the navy-blue meadows to Kara's grave. As he walked through the darkness, with no light but the moon to keep him from veering off the path, he reflected to earlier with Bryant.

***

The moment he choked Bryant, watching the air escape from his body and the blue veins losing their shape, spreading across his face.

Bryant had a dangerous power. He was too unstable to continue walking the city. Bryant reaffirmed it with his self-perspective.

This rage of denying he was a killer. From killing those smugglers back during the adrenaline-fueled blackouts, this was his burden. A heavier burden when he forced Diablo to his death. But that burden soon shattered his mind when he couldn't handle the memory of accidentally killing Kara in his drug-fueled craze.

The idea to remove anyone that labeled him as a killer…became increasingly naïve. Isaac had a conscious will in this decision this time. But, even now, it was a gamble. Would Isaac truly make a difference, or teeter over the edge as a psychopath?

Why continue this downward spiral? Why continue appeasing this insatiable beast of rage? He would be repeating the same incident from more than half a year ago. This wouldn't be something to turn back from but fall further into.

In that split-second moment, where Bryant was close to cracking one last string of air, Isaac roared to dig up more power. He released his grip, and punched Bryant across the face. A force so strong that it batted Bryant's head against the concrete. The lanky teenager snapped back up shaken, caving his chest in, then expanding again as he regained his natural color.

"You don't get to make this decision!" Isaac cried, "You don't have the right to put this burden on ME! YOU live with your choices like I do! Come over here," Isaac pulled Bryant up by the collars, "I'm giving you these choices now: you live your life in New Manhattan where I *never* see you again.

"Or you leave New Manhattan for good or until the day I die, to which, frankly, I *never* encounter you again, and you never the utter words involving me as a killer. And I swear if I ever do cross paths with you again, there won't be an easy way out. I will make your life suffer to an un-imaginable degree."

He moved in closer, roaring from the top of his lungs, "Understand?!"

Bryant nodded rapidly, his mouth agape. Isaac looked down on him, shivering and covered in the dirt of the building's debris. Isaac turned away, leaving Bryant there in the dirt of the dead zone.

***

Isaac made it to the grave, where he sat down with her. But instead of the tragic memories, they were the memories of euphoric nostalgia.

When she took care of him as a child, allowing him to live as a child through water balloon fights, amusement parks, having someone to cry on. And then to support his decision on leaving the mansion years later.

88

Fast-forward to her welcoming Isaac back with open arms after his house burned down. Her choice to help him on his vendetta despite his initial reluctance. "I hope you can understand I never meant to harm you. I still can't remember that entire night. They fucked with my mind so much in the time locked away."

Tiny hills of dirt overlapped one another, surrounding the decomposing bouquets of flowers. And overlapped in Isaac's heart was fear and uncertainty of his choices affecting the future. "I hadn't killed anyone since Diablo. I hadn't made the decision to kill someone again until today. He was dangerous. Unstable with the amount of fucking power he has. I think enough rationale was on the table for me to teeter me over to that edge. He called me a killer. I believed it...so much that it made me furious.

"I had him on his deathbed. This time, I had consciousness. I had clarity. And even with my head being clear, I still don't know if I made the right choice. I don't know if this was the better option.

"I can't change what's happened. I can try to be better than I was before. At least I hope I can. I stopped myself from making life any worse than it could be. But…"

Isaac shifted his attention to the moon. Although he felt

better about this decision, a knot in his stomach lingered once the rage subsided. A warning on whether someone so dangerous should be allowed to walk around this world. If he truly did the right thing by letting him live. He stifled a shout out of frustration, clawing a handful of dirt while trying not to disturb her.

Fog washed over the moon, overlaying the sphere with a panel of frosted glass, blurring the moon's outline. Isaac wiped his eyes. Her warm nature, her unique, caring essence...it swept over into his conscious state of mind. So instant, to keel over and cry over her resting place.

"Fuck, Kara...I'm so sorry. I hope I did the right thing tonight. I'm really…" Isaac's breath shuddered, unable to find the right string of words. "Please forgive me."

Isaac finally uttered her name after half a year. The mass of fog accumulated, forcing the moonlight to dissipate. That night, Isaac slept on frigid blades of grass to keep her company. To keep Kara company.

MAD VIGILANCE

THERE IS NOTHING THAT BRINGS ME MORE JOY IN THE WORLD THAN THIS...

(sans my wife, and universal happiness)

This universe you've entered truly sparks my love for the superhero genre, with the dash of a somewhat grounded atmosphere filled with grit and drama.

There's a lot of excitement bubbling in me as I continue telling stories within the MAD universe, and I can't wait to share them with you.

If you enjoyed Mad Vigilance, then I encourage you to leave a review on Amazon, or wherever platform you may find this novella. One sentence or two makes a difference.

THE STORY CONTINUES

Mad Virus

An infected vigilante. A superpowered terrorist. A virus doomed to devastate the entire world. One chance to do things right.

Available on Amazon.

(Scan the QR code to be taken to the page!)

Since the events of *Mad City*, Isaac Sage has committed himself to the life of a vigilante in an attempt to find full closure over his parents' deaths. With 2 years passed, he's had no luck, aimless even with some outside help. Sage Foundation continues to rise, however, with the introduction of new technologies and the resurgence of M.A.D. compounds beyond the underground market.

But one action can push life towards death's door. When the terrorist Rickard takes advantage of the M.A.D. compound and corrupts it into a virus, infecting New Manhattan, Isaac has only 7 days to defeat Rickard and stop the virus before it spreads into the entire world.

As the clock ticks away, Isaac is harboring his own hidden sins from the past. Sins that question his worthiness to be a hero, or if he's better off rotting to death from the virus. Little does Isaac know that some people may be on this hidden trail, catching up to him.

Can Isaac vanquish his demons, and become the hero necessary to save the world? Or will all his actions be put on the spotlight for the whole world to judge on their last breath?

Mad Virus is the second book of Victor Vahl's MAD series. If you like fast-paced action filled with spices of adventure, thrills, mystery and character-driven drama, then you'll love this installment in Vahl's page-turning series.

BUT WAIT...

Channeling my inner TV salesman to deliver this line: But wait…there's more.

I recall how tedious it sometimes is to find more works written by the same author, after laying one's eyes on their first work and, well, enjoying it!

There are also many who just find it laughably bad and forget the author, moving on to the next. Hey, that happens. If you're one of those people, then happy reading. =)

If you are someone who enjoyed this book, then happier reading! You can find all my other currently published works on my website, linked below.

There is also a newsletter you can sign up for on the website, where you can stay connected with me and check out special promotions, exclusive benefits, behind-the-scenes content, and any other content I find fun to share.

WWW.VICTORVAHL.COM

ABOUT THE AUTHOR

Victor Vahl is a fiction writer specializing in thrillers, dipping in subgenres such as science fiction, action and psychological suspense. His other skills include graphic design, copywriting, video editing and being a self-proclaimed cookie connoisseur. A graduate of Florida State University, Victor Vahl excelled in multiple classes involving creative writing and rhetoric.

Victor constantly finds the opportunity to brainstorm stories (often getting lost in his daydreams) or to research by watching movies and reading books. If it's not any of those things, Victor spends his time by being with his loving wife Mrs. Vahl, petting his dog and cat simultaneously, cooking while struggling to remember the recipe, or just laying in his hammock outside, beneath a cool, gentle breeze.

You can stay connected with Victor Vahl here:

facebook.com/thevictorvahl

twitter.com/thevictorvahl

instagram.com/thevictorvahl

goodreads.com/victorvahl

bookbub.com/profile/victor-vahl